The Silence of Ignited Souls

Compiled By

Akanksha Dhiman and Astha Yadav

BookSquirrel Publication

BookSquirrel Publication

Mahadev Totala Nager, Indore (M.P),452001
Regd Under MSME
Website:
www.booksquirrelpublication.com

"The Silence of Ignited Souls"

By: Astha Yadav and Akansha Dhiman

ISBN: 978-93-89923-89-6

English and Hindi Anthology

Book Formatting: Aryan Verma

Cover Design: Ronak Chavda

DISCLAIMER

This anthology is a work of fiction. The compiler has tried best to edit and curate the content of the co-authors and is made plagiarism free.

In case of any plagiarism detected, neither the compiler, nor the publishers are responsible. Co-authors will be solely responsible for their own content.

<u>ACKNOWLEDGEMENT</u>

The making of this anthology would not have been possible without the co-authors. A gratitude towards all who have worked hard and have made efforts for this book to be a success.

I am thankful to BookSquirrel Publication without whom this project wouldn't have been possible.

Above all, the hearty thanks to my family and friends for supporting me throughout this project. Lastly, I thank the almighty for giving me this opportunity and strength to complete it successfully.

Index

29) Saba Parvez
30) Shivani Tripathi
31) Shivi saxena
32) Sneha Mishra

Astha Yadav

Astha Yadav is a content writer and she has participated in 30+ anthologies as a co-author. Apart from writing, she loves sketching and painting too. She tries to complete her work to perfection. Determination and persistence towards her work will definitely make her successful in future.

Insta id- red_rose431

TO MY BEST FRIEND

I didn't knew, what friendship exactly meant until you
entered my life,
From the day you met,
My life turned to be a heaven on earth.
Today, I want to thank you for everything you did for me.
A mere 'thanks' is not enough to show the gratitude and love
I have for you,
But still,
I want to thank you for never leaving my side even on my
worst days,
Thankyou for dancing for me even if you were not in the
mood,
Thankyou for singing for me though you are not a singer,
But trust me, your voice sounds so melodious to me,
It cures my pain, and vanishes away all my sadness,
Thankyou so much for loving me the way no one ever can,
Thankyou for loving me when I look no less than a chubby
panda,
Thankyou for appreciating me when I feel insecure about
my looks,
Thankyou for motivating me when I start to lose my
confidence,
Thankyou for being my saviour when I mess up everything,
Thankyou for loving me when I am ME.

Akanksha Dhiman

Akanksha Dhiman is an aspiring writer, pursing her passion of writing. She has always been keen to her writing habits. She is a published writer. Her debut book is 'i want to see through your eyes' she is co author of many anthologies. Apart from that she loves to try new things everyday. She has curious mind with optimistic personality. She believes words are important because they are the best way to convey your feelings.

Instagram ID: copper_terillium Failure is not a full stop, it is a box full of experience, hardwork and patience.

A SOUL

A soul tried to bulid up again and again while breaking into pieces of cripples.
Only his arms shows the way to peace
the way moves his fingers on her shattered skin, show her, she can conquer the world just with her smile. Millions of feelings rushed through her vains as his touch disappeared.Her heart skipped a beat right at that second.
Nothing could build her up again instead of his warmth... There he was walking back into the light of his own. Millions of tears craved to drip down her tired skin with just the thought of losing him. As he took his last step, somethimg out of the blue moon forced him to just take a look of her. His stubbornness couldn't last in front of his dispicable heart. Hesitantly his deep browny eyes inspected her with a last hope. His lips couldn't help but give her the last lost gift she deserved from him. A heartwarming smilie holding millions of parts of his heart. His fate even heart knew she's better without his facsimile. She needs to find her Aurora that have no match with his eclipse.

He left her in darkness of old, creppy voices ringed around her as he disappeared into his world. Those voices sounded like nothing but screams of the dead that craved to take her into their world. Even her hands couldn't help her to stop listening to those voices. But... they were too hard ignore in that bizarre place where there was no end of pain and fear. Those voices feed to the fear. She felt their presence through her skin, her senses couldn't lie to her. She was in the middle of nothingness with no end, no beginning. Her heart screamed for the eit from that hell. She could give up on herself... She tried but ended up gaining the courage to fight against the odds. A ray of hope of nothing raised into her. In that short moment of time she became something no one could bear.

She knew she lost her stars just to reach the moon. And she was ready to fight for it at any cost. Those voices around her didn't bothered her anymore, they were too weak to break her believe. She didnt lost herself... that shattered skin of her glowed into the prism of endless pride. She was the dark glowing into the light... The cosmic dark.

Aakansha Bhargava

Aakansha Bhargava has been working with write ups from last 2 years. Her educational background in biotechnology has given her a broad base from which to approach many topics. She not only believe in academics but in reality she wanted to become a leader, because of this she eventually abandoned her academics for write ups. She loves spending time on your quote.

Instagram ID : Akshubhargava_15

एक रोज़

एक दिन बैठूँगी मैं भी
सुनूँगी तुम्हे तुम्हारी हर बात को
तुम्हारे हर ज़ज़्बात को
तुम्हारे हर हालात को

सुनो,
थोड़ा मुझे भी सुनने की कोशिश करना
मेरे भी हाल चाल समझना
कोई भी बुरा नही होता
कोई भी बिका हुआ नही होता
हालात से समझौता करते हुए
हर इंसान नकारा नही होता
बैठूँगी किसी रोज़
तुम्हारी हर बात सुनूँगी
तुम्हारी हर शिकायत सुनूँगी
तुम बताना कितने परेशान हो
तुम बताना कितने हैरान हो
लिखूंगी तुम्हारी हर बात को
तुम्हारे हर सवाल को
समझन ही आएगा
चार-छै: बार पढ़ूंगी
वादा नही करूँगी
ना कोई सवाल करूँगी
बस सुनूँगी तुम्हे

एक रोज़

चले आना मेरे पास
जब तुम्हे लगे हालात
दोनों के ठीक है

The Silence of Ignited Souls

थोड़ा सुनना मुझे
बताना की मैं कितनी ही गलत थी
कैसे मैं तेरी नही बन पायी
जैसी तेरी मैं पहले एक रोज़ थी

तू बताना मुझे
वो हर पुरानी बात को
जो मैंने तेरी गलतियां गिनाई थी
गलत थी मैं भी तेरे नज़रो में
सिर्फ तू अकेला कहाँ खराब था
आना मेरे पास एक रोज़ तू
तेरी बात सुनूँगी
तेरे हर ज़ज़्बात सुनूँगी

Let's talk about the time

When she was young

There's a poetry

On the tip of her tongue

In depression facing agony

She still love her high pony

It's dark in there

No happy surprise

Only this disguise

Of constant lies,

People don't want to bear her

The Silence of Ignited Souls

They want her to hide

They broke her by saying

Just keep your poetry

Empty inside

Lemme take care of my broken heart

N show myself how to fly

Broken wings unable to support me

But I can still reach high in sky

I have a feeling

That I can't comprehend

In my deepest thoughts

You are not just a friend

I just don't need anything to assume

I am broken but I still gift you

Letters with fragrance of my perfume

I always wish that your voice

Would be the last I'd hear

I promise I'd listen attentively

And promise not to shed a tear

Just 1 moment that my heart

Would beat it's last beat

I'd thank the lord for allowing us to meet

अपने वजूद से

दूर खड़ी मैं

पूछ रही थी मेरा पता

जानता है क्या तू

इस शख़्स को

अरे कहीं तो कुछ तो बता

वजूद बोला

मिल जाये तो मुझे भी बताना

न जाने कब से है लापता

दूर खड़ा मैं भी

तलाश रहा हूँ इसका पता

Yes m quite

Not for people m not in touch with

But for people m living in with

Yes m quite

Coz m observing action of people so called mine

Uh know that hurts but m fine

Yes m quite

Knowing our thoughts are not same

But I still laugh on ur Pj's and on ur Lame

Yes m quite

But uh know I need ur hug

It gives warmth and works like piece of rug

Yes m quite

Doesn't means m not noticing fact

It's just I learnt not to act

Adarsh kumar

Hey there it's Adarsh Kumar a student who is with an aim to prove words have emotions

Instagram ID: Adarsh_____ak

The Silence of Ignited Souls

Not always making quick decisions are useful sometimes they
dampen the situation.

The day when you think of giving up

Will be the day after which you can never ever dream of getting up
once again

Trees may fall

Birds may die

Life is a small hall

It's better to be wise

Life is like a book,

If even only few pages are left on your book,

 The pen's ink will be left for an another one.

Not all broken hearts become a bard some move forward in life
and they are the most successful ones.

Adarsh Kumar Singh "Azaad"

My passion, my energy, my drive and my enthusiasm is true, real and undeniable. I don't begrudge anyone who does however.... It's just that's not me. The high I get from creating, writing, conceptualizing and destroying a pepperoni pizza is palpable. I love working with writing skills.

Instagram ID: adarsh.kumar.singh.patel

गुरु

जो कुछ सीखा, सब आप से,

जो कुछ जाना, सब आप से,

जब भी जीवन में एक रास्ता बंद हुआ,

नया दिखाया आपने ,

जब भी दुखी हुए संभाला आपने,

अज्ञान के अंधेरे से, ज्ञान की रोशनी मेंलाया आपने,

इंसान को इंसान बनाया आपने,

जग में एक मुकाम दिलाया आपने,

गुरु आपके उपकार का कैसे चुकाऊं मोल,

लाख कीमती धन भला गुरु हैं मेरे अनमोल।

बैकबेंचेर

स्कूल में दोस्त तो सब बनाते है

लेकिन हम बैकबेंचेर तो कुछअलग ही यादें बनाते है।

क्लास में तो हमारी धाक सी थी

तभी तो क्लास की आखिरी सीट हमेशा हमारे लिए खाली रहती थी।

हम सब को अपना यार मानते थे

बोरिंग लेक्चर्स में भी हम कुछ खुशी के पल तलाश ही लिया करते थे।

The Silence of Ignited Souls

कभी ऑड-इवन तो कभी पेनफाइट हम खेल ही लिया करते थे।

दोस्त का खाना उड़ाने मेंतो हम नंबर वन थे,

टीचर के क्लास में नआने से हम पूरी क्लास को अपने सिर पे उठा लिया करते थे।

टीचर्स के पीछे अजीब-अजीब आवाजें निकालना तो हमारी आदत सी बन गयी थी।

टीचर्स को तो हम बड़ा सताते थे,

फिर उनकी पनिशमेंट से हम भाग भी नही पाते थे।

सबसे ज्यादा मजा तो इंस्पेक्शन के टाइम पर आता था जब हमने एको कॉपी नही बनाई होती थी,

और टीचर्स हमे पकड़ भी न पाते थे।

स्कूल की आधी लड़कियाँ तो हमे भैया कह के बुलाती थी ,

और जो न कहती थी वो हमारी सेटिंग होती थी।

हमारे ग्रुप को तो हम 'स्कूल के लड़ाके' बुलाते थे,

क्योंकि कही भी कोई भी लड़ाई हो हम वहाँ पहुच जाते थे।

स्कूल के रूल्स तोड़ने में तो हमे अलग सा मजा ही आता था,

वो स्कूल में फ़ोन लाना जब हमें मना किया जाता था,

और स्कूल की ड्रेस कभी भी पूरी पहनकर तो हम कभी आते ही नही थे।

पूरी रातभर हम सब दोस्त जागते थे और अगले दिन स्कूल में घोड़े बेचकर सो जाते थे।

आज वह सब हसीन पल याद आते है।

क्यों इतनी जल्दी अलग हो गए हम????

Aftaab Ismail Sonday

Just a simple guy with some meaning words trying to achieve some crazy dreams because for me if my dream is not crazy enough then it's not even in my dream list.

Instagram ID:aftaab_sonday007

Patience will give you true love and forcing will give you regret.

Sometimes you don't get what you love the most because God always try to give you the best and not the one you think is the best because God knows what is better for us and what is not.

Fire makes me believe that as the water makes fire go away one day there will be someone in your life who will work just as same as water and will make all your sadness go away.

Even if I travel the whole world which is actually my dream i am not gonna find a girl as good as you.

Sometimes we don't actually need love we just need the right person to be with us forever.

Ayesha Shaikh

I was born and brought up in the country of Pakistan. From my childhood to my youth, I had always been an ambitious person and a humble human being who has contributed to various occasions, activities, and collaborations for the benefit of society. I aim to mend broken hearts!

Instagram ID: ayeshashaikh9670

Time has a weird way of making us strong, even if we aren't. Natasha came home from school and saw her mother lay unconsciously on the ground. The doctors said she had Alzheimer's disease. It was still in the early stages but it would soon develop and she will forget everything including memories, and names. Natasha knew that her life was never going to be the same again. Her heart broke whenever she'd see her mother forget the people she once loved. Some days, Natasha would comb her mother's hair and someday, she'd whisper hypnotic words of Rumi to her beloved mother because when Natasha was a child, her mother would do the same. Natasha wished for her mother to live. She hoped for all of this to just be a bad dream. She wished to live in a world where they were all together. But this was reality, her mother was dying and there was nothing Natasha could do about it. A life gone too soon, she died in her sleep. At her funeral, Natasha felt numb. That's what happens when you've been heartbroken for long, you don't feel the pain anymore. While cleaning her mother's cupboard, she found a letter which was labelled as "For Natasha", she opened it with a heavy heart and began reading: "I don't have many days to live and I won't stay by your side for an eternity, but please remember one thing "don't let sadness consume your life." I know, things happen, people grow apart. And sometimes, when people grow apart, they walk away from each other but the memories remain. Like a book on a dusty shelf that's been unopened for years. Like that old song, you haven't heard in a while. Sometimes, you remember those memories and you cry, sometimes you smile. That's life, its okay. Learn to live with it. One of the worst feelings about reminiscing old memories is that you look back at all of the times that have passed away, the good and the bad. And it hurts to know that no matter what you do, those moments will never come back again and things wouldn't go back to the way they once used to be. The memories would play in your head like a movie and you'll ache until warm tears fall from your eyes and it's at that moment you realize how much you miss the sound of their laugh and the softness of their touch. Listening to an old song on the radio would remind you of them. You'd go to sleep silently praying for time to turn around so you could experience that feeling all over again, even if it is just for a moment. But the next day, you'll be okay." Natasha felt the paper drop to the floor. And she wept, wailed, sobbed; it's at that moment, she learned the simple truth about life. A perfect life is just an illusion. Her mother was right. She must learn to live with the pain! She'll be okay.

Bibiayeesha Mulla

I am Bibiayeesha Mulla from Karnataka. I love cricket & I am a Chai Lover too. Poetry is my passion & Dentistry is my profession.

Instagram ID: bkmdoc

एक तरफा मोहब्बत

एक तरफा मोहब्बत की बात ही कुछ और होती है बड़ी खास होती है।

एक को बिल्कुल एहसास नहीं तो एक को बस उसकी ही चाहत होती है।

कोई अनजान होता है तो कोई उसके लिए तड़प के रह जाता है।

कदर ना करना मोहब्बत की यह इसका असल मजमून होता है।

कोई जान कर अनजान रहता है तो कोई जान देने को तैयार होता है।

अजीब उसूल है इस मोहब्बत का कोई एक ही इस आग में जलकर रह जाता है।

कभी लोग तमाशा बना देते हैं कभी खुद का ही तमाशा बन जाता है।

मोहब्बत करने वाला बस अपनी मोहब्बत की तलाश में रह जाता है।

किसी की जिंदगी तबाह हो जाती है तो कोई बदनाम हो कर रह जाता है।

मसाला वफा या बेवफा का नहीं इसमें कुसूर मोहब्बत का होता है।

किसी की जिंदगी की वजह तो किसी को बर्बाद कर के रख दिया जाता है।

न जाने क्यों आज भी ये एक तरफा मोहब्बत जिंदा है और रहेगी।

मोहब्बत क्या है?

मोहब्बत वह होती है जिसमें फिक्र होती है।

अपने यार की खुशी में खुद खुश हो जाना।

उसके गम मे उसका साथ कभी ना छोड़ना।

खुद को थोड़ा बदलना जरूरत पड़ने पर।

वक्त आने पर उसे समझ जाना बिना कहे।

उसकी गलती पर रूठ जाना तो कभी माफ कर देना।

बिना झिझक या डर के उससे सब कुछ बता देना।

जिसमें कोई बंदिश ना हो कोई मलाल ना हो।

जिसमें इज्जत सुकून राहत दिल का चैन हो।

इतने अमीर भी नहीं हुए हैं के अपनी मोहब्बत खैरात में किसी को दे आए हम।

इतने गरीब भी नहीं हुए हैं के किसी से अपनी मोहब्बत की भीख मांग आए हम।

ना जाने कैसा असर था उस जालिम की बद्दुआ में यार।

अपना भी ना बनाया और ना किसी और काहोनेदिया।

Chitrotpala Chaitali Dash

Chitrotpala Chaitali Dash has obtained a Bachelor's degree in Biotechnology and hails from Odisha. She is also a writer at buddymantra.com, where she writes various articles under lifestyle and spirituality niches. Chitrotpala's article "Tap into The Power of Magic" was published in the monthly magazine "Infinithoughts" (September 2018 issue). She is a nature-lover, who finds solace in poems and a cup of tea; and believes that we all are made up of stardust and carry a little magic within us.

Instagram ID: chitrotpala_chaitali

THE WARRIOR GIRL - A LOVE TALE

Somewhere across a thousand mile

I met a distant traveler,

Lurked within her mysterious smile

Was a gleam of a triumphal warrior

A girl was she, of peculiar candor

A heart had she, of golden amour

A warrior was she, of bereaved armor

A love had she, of unflinching valor

With a sword in hand sailing the seven seas

In search of love that glossed,

Inside her heart is where she sees

The love that was long lost

Yonder the alp and the abyssal wildwood,

Like a cherry blossoming in childhood,

Was where it dwelled like a shimmering pearl?

The esoteric love tale of a warrior girl.

AN EULOGY FOR MY DIVINE MOTHER

When I sing praises for you

You become the hymn

And reside in its rhyme.

When I meditate on my breath

You become the air

And breathe in and out everywhere.

When I chant your name

You become the thrum

And deep within me, you hum.

When I dance to your tune

You become the beat

And I caper merrily to it.

When I write about you

You become the quill

And your poetry helps me heal.

A POEM IN ME

[34]

When I sit down to write,

A poem bubbles up in me

And ignites in me, a light.

When I lie down and feel,

A poem erupts from my heart

And helps my mind heal.

When I softly close my eyes,

A poem trickles down my cheeks

And mellows my silent cries.

When I think blissfully of you,

A poem twinkles in my eyes

And croons eulogies for you.

Deekshithasowjanyateki

Deekshithasowjanya.Teki Electronics &Communication engg Student also a content writer, etymologist, poetess.

Instagram ID: deekshith_teki

Dear Stranger,

From Dark to bright

The torment passes right.

I hanged out like shingle,

To make myself bright.

I believed myself

Because I am with good intentions.

No dice! Nitty - Gitty

It's like a needle in the hay stack..

From dark to bright

The torment passes right.

.

.

Left with pain.

Brokenhearted

Little pitchers have big ears ..
As little hearts have big thoughts..
But,my hands are tied when I try to explore..
I tried to gain my emancipation..
Realized that Rome was not built in a day..
Heard a call to sing for a supper..
Dedicated whole life to look for his stay.

Love yourself

I heal myself with ink
Letting the paper go wet
AS I CRY
I heal myself with ink
As skeleton is so close
TO MY EYE
I heal myself with ink
As snug as a bug in a rug
IN SIGHT
I heal myself with ink
As I spilled the beans to the WRONG PERSON
I heal myself with ink
To purely
BE MINE

दीपक अनंत राव "अंशुमान"

Deepak Anantha Rao (M.A,M.Phil,B.Ed,)
Govt.High School Teacher. Kerala

पुरुषार्थ मेरा, बहु तुम्ही से हो पूरी

जब मैं अपने घर आता हूँ,

देहरी पर मुस्कान लिए मेरी देवी होगी।

प्यार की पंखुडियाँ सी मेरे सीने पे,

सदा खिलने वाली मेरी प्रियतमा होगी।

वह मेरी बहु,

दर्द की काण्टे दिल पर चुभ कर तडपता हूँ।

अपनी फूलों जैसे मुलायम ऊँगलियों से वो,

मेरी बहु, उन काण्टों को बहार बना देती।

क्षमा में वह घरती है, रुप में वह लक्ष्मी,

कर्म में वह दासी, कार्य में वो मंत्रि,

वह मेरी बहु।

कभी भी न बुझने वाली दीप है वो,

मेरे साथों जनम की अन्न दाता है वो,

साया बनकर मुझमें समाया रागणि है वो .

मेरे तकदीर का रूपक है वो।

मेरे कवित्त का अनूठा रस है वो,

प्यार से पिरोये शब्दों की छडी है वो,

बहू तू कभी बनती माता है मेरी,

बहन की छवी भी झलकती तुम्ही पर।

सफर में सदा तू हमराह बनती,

सासों में रहते है गर्मी तुम्हारी,

पलकों के नीचे तू ही रहेगी,

बहु तुझसे बनती है जीवन हमारी।

पिता बन गया हूँ सफर मेरी जारी,

बहु की यह माहिमा कभी न होगी पूरी।

पुरुषार्थ मेरा सिर्फ, तुम्ही से हो पूरी

सुन लें बहु ये सब मेहरबानी तुम्हारी॥

चिथडे जिस्म की वो आवाज़ रही तू

तू आस मायिश थी मेरी,

पलकों में भरे ख्वाहिश थी,

हर रातों में, अकेली बातें में

तेरा ही फरमाइश थी,

पौरों तले तुम्हारी ही श्रृंगार थी,

बदन में खिली कोमल फूल तेरी छवि थी,

मनमानी करती रागिणी थी,

खुद को बना द्रूँलहराती सितार थी,

पिरोये यादों की बारात तू थी,

दिल की दरिया के अघ खुली कली थी,

हर फासलों में करीब तू ही थी,

यहाँ मेरी जीने की कला नूही थी,

बस तुमको देखा मैं चाहा तुम्ही को,

बसते रीबोली में अटकी हुई हूँ,

गहरा अन्धेरा जो मुझपे बिखेरा

तो जलती छलकती दिया तूही थी,

अब मेरी राहों में काण्टें बिझी है,

तू मेरे जीवन में अब ना रही है,

कुछ पाके, कुछ खो के जीवन बचा हूँ।

खायी कसम थी, तू उस दिन जो मुझसे,

क्या हो गई थी कसम वो तुम्हारी,

भूली हुई वो दास्तान तुम्हारी,

पिघलती है यादें एक बार फिर मुझमें।

एक दिन चली तू मुझको रुलाके,

ए दर्दे दिल तू ज़रा संभाल मुझको,

यह बदन सी बकी आशियाना यही थी

चिथडे जिस्म की वोआवाज़ों रही तू।।

Divyasree

Pessimistic brain in an optimistic soul, Photography enthusiastic, Procaffeinator, Philanthropic.

Instagram ID: Div._.yaaa_

The Silence of Ignited Souls

In the vicious cycle of life,

With sun beautifully shinning and the birds chirping

Moving along with the race of life, my eyes stopped at the moment I caught her eyes.

It's that the moment I realised that not every story needs to be a fairy tale, a fragile story can be inspirational too.

It told me several stories which I could perceive.

I could see this little girl

Struggling with her little story.

It was nostalgic to me on seeing this onlooker, with shinny pretty eyes and lots of dreams to me achieved.

I was curious in knowing her story, curious because we had a similar story line, with different context.

Lost in my thoughts, I could see her dad running towards me with a fall of hope. Her dad was not like how the superheroes we presume to be, but for her he's the superhero.

Even though he was broken physically, he had hopes that his daughter should not face the same.

His daughters eyes were prettier than we could ever imagine - filled with dreams, stories, love and lots of fun.

But the world failed to see what I saw in her. Her eyes was squinted.

The story I could see was similar, because even though we are moving forward with the society and world, it seems to be the same till date. Bullying is been a part of the life and children are not aware of what harm it could cause thier fellow mates.

I could feel the pain she was going through, so I just hugged on seeing her. But her reaction seemed to be different, different than I could ever presume. She just smiled and gave a huge hug back.

I curiously asked her what's the reason behind the smile.

She told," it's a little secret, do you want to know?" I just nodded my head.

She continues saying, "world is too big to understand what others are thinking, everyone has a story - find yours!!"

Those lines just inspired me.

I wish I could have had the courage just like that little girl

Geethika.A

Geethika.A Of age 19 being studying bachelor's of interior design and decoration in jd institute of fashion technology is very creative in aspects like designing, writing, photography and many more. Would like to be a recognized person as much as possible with all my means of contact to people. Please do give your encouragement. Thank you.

Instagram ID:_geetha_naidu_

Everything and everyone against you

The Silence of Ignited Souls

Hearts who loved are gonna leave you

Pains started treating you.

Social media feels like a medicine at your bad times rite?

But remember high dosage may kill you.

Today's world behaves like..

Questioning eyebrows lifting up

Shocked eyelashes flapping down

Helpless eyes standing still.

Life which we live

Cradle to grave

Is filled with human crave.

May be your eyes filled

With problems acts like a magnet.

But surely my heart filled

With pain won't attract like an iron.

Harshita Singh

It's Harshita singh. I am a student of engineering and I do writing as it makes me feel calm. In future if possible I love to be a good writer.

Instagram ID:atihsrah_singh &words_with__emotion

Vaise th ishq mujhe hi nhi unhe bhi hua hi tha mujhse,

Vaise th ishq mujhe hi nhi unhe bhi hua hi tha mujhse...

Aisa kisi Roz kaha tha unhone

Aisa bhi nahi tha ki sirf mere chahre pr muskaan aa jaaya
Karti thi unhe dekh kar,

Uss muskaan ko dekh kr unki bhi th saanse tham si jaaya
karti thi...

Aisa jataya bhi th tha unhone

Haa haa yaad hai mujhe Jb tm kaha krte the ki mil jaaenga
bahut tumhe bhale hi mujhe chedne k liye, tb main sirf
itna kha Karti thi ki " pyaas th Paani se bhujhti hai, jaam se
nhi"....

TB tm mujhe pagal kh kr thoda muskura bhi th diya karte
the ar ek pyaari si thapki bhi th lga diya karte the...

"Kudh k chaand ar mujhe uss chaand ki chaandni bhi th
bta diya karte the....

Dil se roe pr hothon se muskura baithe,

Yu hi hm unko apna bana baithe....

Vh hamari mohabbat se mohabbat tk n kr paae

Ar hm unke liye apni zindagi luta baithe....

Main jo kisi din gahri neend main so jau,

Th Tm jara sa bhi mt ghabrana...

Aankhon main aansun nhi tm chahre pr muskaan banae
rakhna,

Aree pagal kahi jaake aaj th neend muqambal hui hai....

Heet Shah

Writer scribblings thoughts with a hope to express myself to the world through some words. Extremely grateful for the Loving ones in my life, they are truly my source of inspiration. Adventurous heart and a serene mind.

Instagram ID:immature_voice

हा ये वही नारी हैं

जिन्हे तुम तेवहारो के दिन पूजते हो

और अगले दिन इन्हे जलील करते हो,

हा ये वही नारी हैं

जो कहीं तुम्हारे मां के रूप में

कहीं तुम्हारे बेहेन के रूप में

तो कहीं तुम्हारे सहेलियों के रूप में तुम्हे दिखेगी,

इन्हे भी हक्क मिलना चाहिए अपने सपनों के पंख से उड़ने का,

पर ना मिला हक्क ना इज्ज़त क्युकी ये औरत हैं,

जब एक नारी की शक्ति के सामने युमलोक के राजा झुक्क सकते हैं,

तो हम तो फिर भी इंसान हैं,

कभी ना समझना कि यह अकेली क्या करेगी

यह अकेले ही हर मुसीबत पर भारी पड़ेगी,

महिलाओं को इतनी आजादी मिलनी चाहिए कि वो अपना रास्ता खुद तय करे,

कि वो खुद ही अपनी खुशी की ज़िम्मेदार हो,

अपने सारे सपने पूरे करने के लिए अपने समय का इस्तेमाल कर पाए,

जिस जगह नारी हो वहा कांटे भी फूल बन सकते हैं,

यह कहा जाए वहा खुशियों की सौगात ले आए,

ये दुनिया भागे लक्ष्मी के पीछे पर ये भी नाजाने की लक्ष्मी तो अपनी ही बेटी हैं,

महिलाएं असल में समाज की वास्तुका रहोती हैं,

जो समाज को एक रहने लायक जगह बनाती हैं,

झुक्क कर नमन करो इन्हें जिनके होने से आज हम हैं।

Marrying you was the only dream that i saw and which stayed constant everytime,

Everytime i just thought of was just being permanent guy in your life being that one guy you could trust your life with,

Just made myself so much prepared for that one thing i always dreamt of and being with you holding your hand throughout my life till we have wrinkles on our face n still love each other forever.

उन्न खुले मैदानों जैसा हर पल हवा की तरह तुम्हे छूना चाहता हूं,

उन्न बाघों के फूलों पर भवरों की तरह तुम्हारे साथ अपनी पूरी जिंदगी बीताना चाहता हूं,

उन्न शर्मीले पत्तों की तरह तुम्हारे छूने से यूं शर्माना चाहता हूं,

बस ये एक ही तो ज़िंदगी हैं मेरे पास और उसे भी तुम पर कुर्बान करना चाहता हूं।

Ishani Agarwal

Ishani Agarwal, born and brought up in Kolkata, she has done her schooling and college from here itself. She is doing her post-graduation at the moment. Ishani loves talking to people around, and is excited for this new beginning of hers! Been a Compiler for 10+ Anthologies and in the process for more, also, Co-authored in 30+ Anthologies,
Ishani is very happy with how her life is turning out now!

Instagram ID: Ishani_agarwal_quotes

SCARY DREAMS...

Waking up wet every morning,
She did not know what was wrong with her..
All day, intimidated by her husband,
All evening it was her kids who would rule on her..
And all night, these dreams would kill her from within..
She was once the topper of her class...
It was love that made her lose focus and direction..
And today ?
She cannot even hold the pen properly to sign..
For her, she believes her dreams are better than reality..
At least, she can kill herself in them.
Here, she is alive from outside, and dead inside...
Are her dreams more scary? Or her reality??

Feminism...

All of us talk about it...
But how many believe it?
Is it real?
Does it exist?
Questions questions...
If you think about it, it does exist!
If you don't think about it, it doesn't...
Why do you need to talk about it separately?
Isn't all the same?
Once, you need equality, and then, you want feminism...
Feminism is something, that is there embedded in our hearts, coz
that is what we learn..
But for me, feminism is a myth...
It is just in our minds.
In reality, feminism does not exist for me...

Time..

This word kept going on and on in her head..
Time is what she did not have..
But, she did not want to tell this to her children..
Diagnosed with leukemia, this free women got into a lot of stress...
The most shocked were her kids,
Who had always lived with their nanny, due to lack of time from
their mother..
But now, she would be always available for them...
Taking them to classes,
Having meals with them,
Playing with them..
Talking to them all day..
This was the most the kids had seen of their mother..
When she knew her condition got worse,
She gave away her kids to her sister to care for,
And she felt a strange kind of ease in her chest..
After spending so much time with her kids, she had no more
regrets left in life.
She died a very peaceful death..
As for her kids,
They now had a very beautiful memory of their mom.. not a one
full of hatred anymore..
It is rightly said, nothing is greater than time.
Earlier, the expensive gifts she would get them, the high end
facilities she gave them,
Is not what the children remember now..
All they remember is the time they spent with their mom...

Janhvi.jaiswal

I am just a words of your, passionate to write and love to giving words to thoughts and try to connect to others with that, I can feel your emotions hope you can feel my words.

Instagram ID: janhvi.jaiswal

The Silence of Ignited Souls

You make me awake the whole night even I am comfortably sleeping in my bed.

You are running all the time in my head.

Is something happened to me or like people said; it's nothing you are just getting mad.

You are so far from me then why I feel so close, like all the shades of red are rose.

It just a illusion of my mind or a magic of yours; please help me out from all this chaos.

Maybe you are good looking or maybe you are not, maybe you are funny or maybe you are not.

If I ever fall for you, I also fall with all your flaws because at the end only you matter for me baby nothing else at all.

Your late reply also give me a false hope.it make me believe that the next day you gonna talk more.

The Silence of Ignited Souls

Even I saw your ignorance but my heart says, you might be
busy; to forget all my efforts its not that much easy.

This is not real it's all imaginary,

Maybe what I feel is just temporary.

I know you belong to the world

Which is outside of my boundaries but I don't know why,
I'm still hoping for contrary.

Kaustubh Pandey

कौस्तुभ पाण्डेय युवा पीढ़ी के उभरते हुए लेखक एवं कवि हैं। प्रतापगढ़ उत्तर प्रदेश के बेनीपुर ग्राम में जन्मे कौस्तुभ विभिन्न सामाजिक मंचों पर अपनी राय तथा कवितायें रखते रहे हैं। वे विशेष रूप से सामाजिक विषयों पर लिखते हैं।

Instagram ID: Indian_pen

जुर्म और आँसू

क्या लिखूँ जो बयाँ करे इस क्लिष्ट विषैली बात को

सम्मान लुट गया भारत की इक बेटी का उस रात को

वो तो इतनी दयावान थी , जानती थी कि दर्द में परिंदे भी होते हैं

कहाँ पता था उसको कि समाज में दरिंदे भी होते हैं

भारत की गरिमा चीखी होगी, संस्कृति होगी चिल्लाई

जब उन गंदे कीड़ों ने होगी दामन पर कालिख लगाई

आँखों से बरखा टपक पड़ी है

उभर उठी चिंता रेखा

आज सुबह जब अखबारों में इंसानियत को मरते देखा।

अटल बिहारी वाजपेयी

वे शताब्दी के सूरज थे

इस नवयुग के निर्माता थे

वे सूरज थे इस भारत के

परमाणु भारत के प्रणेता थे

इस युग के रत्न समान वे

भारत रत्न के धर्ता थे

राजनीति के शीर्ष पुरूष

वे अटल विश्व के नेता थे।

मैं नव पुष्प आज आज इस बगिया में

कविता की रचना करता हूँ

हे कवि तुम्हारे अटल व्यक्तित्व की सप्रेम अर्चना करता हूँ

माँ सरस्वती के चरणों में विनम्र वंदन करता हूँ

अपने इस नवकाव्य संग्रह का हल्दीचंदनकरताहूँ।

Kishore Yadav

I am Kishore Yadav, a data analyst by profession and a passion writer who finds solace in words

Instagram ID: _____yadav_____

Dear father,

I know you are old now, I can see your shoulders falling, you losing your mussels and your anger mellowing down.

Just remember here I am to shoulder you for eternity, for you have sheltered me with the same for these many years.

Just sit down and relax and see how your son is gonna build a kingdom around you

For all you thought me, all you said to remember and from all the mistakes you corrected me

Here i am ready to continue your reign, never feel aged because u leave in my actions as me to be your shadow

You shall always stay my strength & my hero,

I am all that you sacrificed

Your son

When I am not able to write I am stuck inside my head with millions of thoughts, thousands of fears, hundreds of regrets and one soul trying to break free.

Myfavoritemistake,

Your presence brings color to my life,

Your face is like the sun, without which my day never begins

Your smile is the sunshine that speeds my day

The Silence of Ignited Souls

Your eyes are the reflections of my greatest dream that pushes me
to work

Your touch is all the reason why my senses exist

Your warmth is what that's keeping me in the balance of the
hardships of life...

And you are on the whole the reason for my existence...

Thanks for being as you BEE...

A fortress built upon small small memories and unconditional love,

Shaken by the complexity of its residents,

Only way to ensure its existence is to abandon it and move to a far
view point,

And cherish that's my achievement

May be you did not get to experience it, but you get to see it stand
with pride and joy of itself and its residents,

Isn't it what the heart wanted?

To see it's interest cherish with joy,

It's all worth that smile..

It's all true love and care ever meant...

#good_bye_is_always_better_than_get_lost

Build your kingdom first then search for the queen, because she
deserves it...

Mohammad Fazal Shams Christu

Fazal Shams Christu, is a graduate in Commerce. He is a positive thinker and likes to live in his own imaginary world. One day his heart told him to become a 'Best Filmmaker', so he is working towards his goal. His insta id @fazalchristu0127 you can ping him there any time for filmy gossips.

Instagram ID: fazalchristu0127

Bow-Wow...I'm scared of it..!!

"Mr. Shuklaji... When is it going to complete" he asked from the house builder who has designed the building and the construction work was going there. They were some distance away from the site.
"Namstey....Sahabbjii. (Hello sir). It is going to complete sooner. Everything is going according to the plan...Just look at it" he showed the paper which he was holding. He looked at it; it was structure of the building drawn on the paper and then he looked over the construction area. He found that the work is up to the plan and passed smile to him.
"Impressive....There is some magic in your hand. I have heard about your work from many people" he praised his and that house builder, Shuklaji, also felt proud.
"But one thing more Shuklaji" his tone was serious now.
"What..?? Just tell me...Sahabji??" Shuklaji replied. He got worried thinking that he had mistakenly done something wrong. He was very famous for constructing all types of houses in that area.
"Don't worry, your work is very good, I want only one favor from you that is please complete all the work till twenty-one. If you needed some more co-workers than tell me" he joined his hand in front of him; he was looking very wealthy person but yet he begged which showed his simplicity. Shuklaji stopped him.
"Sahaab (Sir) we will try but don't do this" he was feeling guilty by his behavior. "Today is five, enough time but more workers will be needed, I will tell you in the evening about the entire requirement" he spoke loud as that guy walked some feet ahead to look over the work.
He nodded and walked more closely to the construction area and looked each and every thing very clearly. He talked with some co-workers and guided them too. He wanted to complete all the work before twenty-one. He had some plan in his mind. He knew constructing something in area of over 5,000 sq. ft. needed more time still he wanted it sooner.
He walked out of the place. He was getting late; he had to reach his work place in twenty minutes. He was owner of one of the famous restaurant in his city, that restaurant had many branches in the city and in other cities too.
As he was going to seat in his luxurious car, he found something unusual behind his car. He saw that a dog was crying; his voice was too loud. The

dog was looking very weak and very thin in appearance. He felt very sad for the dog and called his driver to feed him.

When that dog ate the food, he wagged his tail to the right, a dog sign, which means he was very happy by the food. That guy also felt good, smiled and sat into his car & the car started moving.

He took his phone lying on the seat. He found that there were ten missed calls and all of them were from his wife. He called back.

"Hey! Stupid... What happened? Don't call me that much otherwise..I will stay home all the time" he said romantically; he loved his wife more than anything.

"Are bewkoof (Stupid)..!!? You forget your important documents at home. You turned too much careless from some days. Don't know what happened to you" as he looked over his seat he quickly asked from his driver for the documents and found that he had really forgotten his important documents. He was going to sign a deal regarding his new branch of the restaurant. He told his driver to go home.

He reached and picked his documents and listen some words from his wife for free. "I don't know what you are doing these days. You are always lost in your thoughts don't know why.. You are hiding something from me……..if you have some problems with me, you can tell me easily" she said him when he was leaving and didn't responded. This made her more worried about him. She knew his behaviors from many years but the way he was behaving, it was unacceptable for her.

He didn't tell her wife about this new dream project. The reason only knew by him, in addition he also warned his driver and all his workers not to tell his wife about this new building that he was constructing. It was secretly creating.

He reached his office, his new branch got approved and it was going to open soon. He done all the legal requirements same day; he was too much busy that he didn't know when the clock hits ten. He was coming back to his home; he stopped at a famous tea stall to drink some tea. It was in his routine. He was standing out of his car and there were complete silence. His driver ordered and later served it to him; he was drinking tea by taking support of his car's bonnet.

His eyes were on the road and he was thinking something. He also saw that a dog was sleeping in the middle of the road. After few seconds, he heard some music and he looked back. He saw that a car was coming at a very high speed with full volume of the speaker; it was interpreting that the driver was drunk. They didn't honk and tried to run over the dog sitting there. That dog quickly stood up and saved his life from death or any kind of damage to him. All the dogs, maybe his friends, got emotional and started barking aloud. That guy was seeing all these; the stupidity of humans over animals.

When he sit back in the car and his driver went toilet he also noticed that whenever some car were going at a high speed from there they will bark like they will eat them but they really don't want this; they only want that the humans should slow down their car speed when they see some dogs sleeping or seating on the road. They don't have houses like humans, they have only road to sit and sleep and even they don't have foods to eat. Nobody is helping animals. Everybody will put some stories or status on their social media showing that they love animals but in really they don't really care in fact they are burden by doing this nonsense activities.

The driver came back start the car and in few minutes they were home. He was tired and he ate dinner quickly served by his wife; he also noticed that his wife was not talking with him. He was thinking about his project while eating & didn't try to ask what had happened to her. His wife got angrier,"I'm going to sleep. If you need something more just take it by yourself, I'm very tired, I need some rest...Ookk fine....byeeee" she told in a rude voice and started moving into their room.

He laughed at her. He was laughing at her cuteness; she always looks cute when she gets angry, according to him. He completed his dinner and he knew than that if he will not talk with her now, the matter will become worse. And actually he wanted to have a talk with her regarding to the incident of the dog earlier that night.

When he entered the room, he can clearly listen her sobbing. She was crying by covering her face with the blanket. He got worried as he always cared for her but from some days he was hiding something from her, he wanted to tell her but still kept it as a secret from her for some reasons.

He removed her blanket, she was trying to escape and he holds her into his arms and hugged her tightly. "I'm sorry yrrr...Please forgive me' he told her in a sweet voice like he always does with her when she got sad. She hugged him while scolding, "I knew you have not changed...You are doing this things just to disturb me…Its okk…now tell me what are you hiding with me" she said and they were still in each other's arm.

As he listened this his expressions got changed, he didn't want to speak the truth so he changed the topic. "You were right….Dogs don't bark unusually they are having some reasons behind their behavior..I was fool I always afraid of them, thinking them as a bad creature" he told looking into her eyes shamefully. She asked her what he was saying and he explained that incident fully when he was drinking tea.

"I told you duffer.. You never knew that...Dogs are the cutest animal. If you respect them, they will respect you. If you try to mess with them like that drunk guy they will bark and eat you..Hhahahhah.." she explained everything about the dogs in her cute voice and rubbed his cheeks while laughing at him. She knew better that how much he scare from the dogs since his childhood. He was listening her silently and again started thinking about his project deeply.

"Buttt…you know..?? I love it that you have some phobia regarding dogs..and ask me why??" she told to broke his silence. "Whyyy" he replied absently.

"If you haven't afraid of dogs we haven't met each other and haven't fallen for each other to get married" she said happily, his attention returned. He laughed back and they started their conversations.

"I never knew that you were living in my colony though…. where I came as a tenant, I'm very thankful to our colony dogs, if they haven't barked at me whenever I was coming late at night you haven't walked out of your house and if you haven't walked out of your house to help me that night I haven't heard your voice and wasn't fallen for you" he said while remembering how they met each other for the first time.

They were living in the same colony and he didn't know until that day when a dog started barking at him continuously while he got afraid and started shouting. He always afraid of dogs, reason he never knew.

Whenever he was coming late at night from some party as college going guy what actually do; partying late at night, the street dogs barked at him.

One day when he was coming back from party he was alone and his bike got punctured before the starting of his colony and he started walking with his bike. Suddenly some dogs started barking, it was their normal behavior when they bark at somebody in night it is their own trick to figure out the thief and dogs are expert in it but he got scared too much that he started running with his bike and dogs also run behind him barking; anyhow he saved himself from them. When he reached his home, he promised himself that he will never do late night party again. But again he did this.

One day again, he came back from party drop his friend at his house and started moving alone. He had forgotten that day that he scare of dogs. He started driving at high speed and when dogs, who are sitting in the middle of the road, saw this they started barking at him so that he can slow his speed. But he never tried to understand them, he always feared of them and in fear he raised his speed more. One of the dogs was stubborn and started running behind him while barking loudly. He was raising his accelerator and the dog was accelerating his legs, as his bike was very old it stopped in few moments.

 His body started shivering in fear and that dog was continuously barking at him. He didn't let him to move an inch; whenever he tried to take a single step he stopped him by barking. He was feeling hopeless he thought that the dog either was going to bite him or not letting him to go. The over thinking led him to shout, "Help.!!.help.!!.Please somebody can help me..pleaseee…"

At one of the houses where he stood with his bike, someone came at their roof and noticed his shouting, it was a beautiful girl. She looked at him and recognized him as she saw him many times and were very impressed by him from many days.

She run down from the roof and came out of the house in minutes, "don't worry be relax, stop shouting" she told him from the backside. Her voice was cuter like girls announcing news in the radio. He turned back and in few seconds his fear left as he got mesmerized by her beautiful appearance. She was a slim girl with beautiful childlike voice.

She was holding a packet of biscuits in her hand and she threw some of them on the other side of the road. The dog roared at her but she didn't fear and she sang something, kind of songs that dogs are liked and threw some more biscuits there. This time he got there and started eating. By the time, he was seeing her activity and enjoying the scene.

"Now you can go…he will not bark at you…but go slow" she gave her this suggestion.

"Okk..but..thank you very very much..if you haven't come.. I would have been stuck here all the night" she blushed at his reply.

"It is my pleasure to help my colony people" she said in a flirty way as she liked him very much. They had some talks and exchanged their name. He went house and at same day he send her friend request and the same day he read her bio in which it was clearly written.
 'I'm a dog lover. I love them feeding and taking care of them. I want to create a place where I can serve every street dog of my city.. PLZ GODDDD..!!...make my wish come true'

....

21, the day finally came. All the construction was done and it was ready as per the plan. He came with his wife, her eyes were covered with black cloth and he took her to the main gate of that building, it was decorated with red tapes and was ready to inaugurate.
He told her to open her eyes. As she opened her eyes she got surprised by seeing all the things. In addition to beautiful decoration, something more were beautifully written on the main gate.
'HaPpY BirThdaY Swthrt...!' she got emotional and tuned to her right side to react. As she turned, she didn't found him.
"Where are you looking? I'm here" he told her while bending down to his knees. She looked at him. "Don't cry. Just accept this" it was a box wrapped like a gift. She opened it and found a key. She didn't understand it.
"What's this??" she asked from him confusion. "Key to open the door of this building" he told smiling. She started looking at the building. She raised her eyes above and read the name of the building written there.
'Dog Villa- A home of Street Dogs'
She hugged him excitedly as her childhood dream finally came true.

Mebitha Lordlin Kiruba M

Adaptable yet Anchored.

Instagram ID:Mebithalkm

Open

Its pitch dark

I turn and spin

There's no spark

To come over and win

It's just cozy

Wherever I place my head

There I feel woozy

Not knowing where I'm led

It's been months and days

I kept swirling

There're no feasible ways

But just whirling

There came a light

I saw someone so massive

With a smile so bright

But I felt passive

Of feeling just awoken

I heard a whisper unbroken

Proclaiming

The world is wide open

And you are the chosen!

Hearing that with a happy sigh

The new born let out her first cry!

Naman (Ankita+Namita)

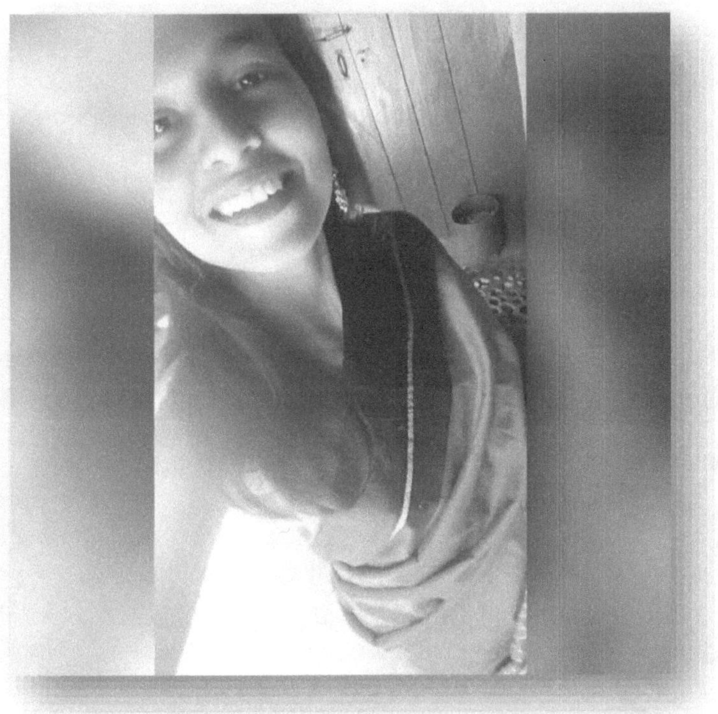

Ankita, a brown girl who never cared about society's opinion towards her. Tender calm and cheerful outside with traces of craziness. Still exploring the world of writing by mingling words with her own unspoken imagination. Writes a lot, not a writer though.

Instagram ID: cinnamino_sticko

The Silence of Ignited Souls

Under the night sky where stars are bridesmaid

And this green meadow is where our marriage is being portrayed

I promise you a sweet kiss of togetherness

Along with a hug of wilderness

That our love would cherish forever

With the trust that would vanish never.

Blessed with the moon,

Without being traditional bride and groom.

Feels like God gave boon without any rituals and customs

Because He knew that for an inter-caste marriage, society would
never loosen its systems.

Hope is a fire in a dead cold town,

It is a gem to a new King's crown.

Hope is that light in which tiny desires survive.

Hope is that lamp which keeps the fire of faith alive.

Hope is a path finder to a failure's goal.

Hope is a thirst to a passionate soul.

Hope is someone's strongest trait,

Hope is other's weakest bait.

Hope is a mirror to everyone who stares.

It lies in the heart of one who prays.

The Silence of Ignited Souls

While the protagonist in the movie kissed his dead lover to bid a
goodbye,

He too kissed her with wet eyes.

Hugged her and whispers

Promise me that you'll stay with me forever!

She calm him down with slap

Shouting, "Idiot I'm the safest creature in your lap."

Both of them laughed knowing that they are constant for each
other,

Without caring about the destiny or whatever!!!

Namita

I am a girl, I am just another dreamer like you, who is on a mission of removing biogtry and hate from the heart of people .I love writing and reading about space and Universe. I look forward to having as many stamps as possible on my passport.

Instagram ID: that_summer_dream

WE MADE THEM BLIND

Me,you, WE made them blind .Made them blind by calling out nasty names for the things they can't even change.That pretty girl whom you called fatso that day in canteen just to hide your own insecurities, she is starving herself to death these days.That intelligent guy you and your boys locked and teased yesterday in that old hostel room just for of a little fun,he wants to commit suicide because of all the humiliation he has to face every other day.That gay couple who was mocked in college campus few days ago by some intolerant people, they are scared ;scared of showing love and spreading love . That girl who lives next door wears makeup every single day because she no longer feels beautiful in her brown skin.They all overthinking day and night,overanalyze every single flaw because we have pushed them soo far. We made them believe they are ugly and they should hate every single inch of their body.It's not just you , it's not just me,we as a society made them believe that they are not worthy of love and happiness.

For once let me be your mirror, let me tell you your stretchmarks are your battle scars and that little gap between your teeth makes your smile more beautiful. Trust me, love comes in all the different forms, shapes and sizes and be it brown, black, pale every skin colour is equally beautiful. Let me tell you, I understand you don't trust anyone anymore after being bullied but there are good people in this world who genuinely cares. I know it's difficult to believe but chivalry is not dead yet and humanity is still breathing. I wish I could tell you this not just today but every single day, that beauty goes deeper than the surface. You are beautiful for having a giving heart and a pure soul. You are beautiful for being kind to others and you are beautiful for giving them helping hands even though you yourself were drowning. You are beautiful for being strong and you are beautiful for smiling even when you were hurting.You are beautiful with all your flaws ,with all your curves and your quirks.Most importantly you are beautiful for being YOU,and trust me love you are worthy of all the love and hapiness in this universe .

THAT ONE QUESTION

17 December 2012,
This date is still imprinted on my mind as it was the beginning of it all . This was the very day when that question came to my mind and never left . I was 13 ,a curious and very talkative girl whose maths book flashed the number 8. I didn't

wanted to come out of blanket on that freezing winter morning but my mom kept shouting " Wake up ! Else you will be late again ." I stepped on the ice cold floor and looked out of the window , everything was covered in dense fog . My little money plant had little dew drops on it , I wondered if it was crying too ? Then I laughed at my own thoughts and said , "Come on ! He doesn't even have to give any maths test , there is no reason for him to be sad ." Yes , I had a maths test today ,and I was anxious .

I left my room and peeped into kitchen where my mom was standing with a glass of warm milk . I quickly turned my back and ran to my dad ,he was taking his daily dose of news from "Dramatic Indian News Channels." I hugged him but today his eyes couldn't leave the television screen . I sat besides him and my mom came to with a military order to finish that glass of milk in 30 seconds . Suddenly my dad 's phone rang and he said it's a public holiday ,which means NO school and NO maths test . I was beaming with joy , loosened my hair , threw my socks in opposite corner of rooms and was going to take my blanket from my room but suddenly a line on television grabbed my attention , " A girl brutally raped in South Delhi " . My feet went backwards and eyes on the screen . Yes , I got a holiday that day , reason being Nirbhaya rape case .My eyes were glued to that screen and I was terrified and confused listening to every word they were saying . I turned to my mom and asked " What is this word ? It's always on newspaper , always on TV , what exactly is Rape ? " My mom told me it's a crime against humanity and sighed .

Crime against humanity ? These words made home in my heart and whole day I was restless . I opened that classic Oxford dictionary and looked for this strange word. I took my dad 's phone and dived deep and my heart sank seeing the results , just one voice came out of my mind , "WHY WOULD SOMEONE DO SUCH AN OBNOXIOUS THING ? " . I was terrified .

On the very next dawn , I was anxious again because of the same maths test . I wore my red sweater and new pleaded grey skirt that my mom bought yesterday from that uniform store . Our bus didn't came that day and my brother was staying home . Me and a friend ,who was older than me , decided to take a risk that day . Yes a big risk in India . We decided to take a public transport . I was very happy about it , my eyes were glowing because I assumed it's the first step on my journey of being a independent girl . On that freezing winter morning , on our way to the school I was explaining her every horrific detail about this thing called " Rape " . Suddenly I felt a cold touch on my right

The Silence of Ignited Souls

knee .It just felt soo wrong. It was a muddy hand rubbing my knee trying to get inside that new beautiful grey skirt . Every single cell of my body froze and my brain become numb , I couldn't speak a single word . A moment ago I was uttering words after words and a moment later there was a painful silence . My eyes suddenly filled with tears and next thing I remember was my friend shouting at him in a rage . That terror I felt just yesterday became my reality . My heart was shattered in million pieces thinking about the sea of pain and fear Nirbhaya must have dived in but my mind was still shouting , " WHY WOULD SOMEONE DO SUCH AN OBNOXIOUS THING ?"

I followed that case closely and would pray for death penalty on every hearing . As the case got new hearings , I encountered new cases of harrassment . I was being stalked , eve teased ,forced and even touched by a teacher . Days , months and years passed , getting new dates use to feel like a mundane routine , so are these petty incidents that were happening more often . Every year I encountered a new Nirbhaya contrived to death , followed by candle march and nation wide protests and every day I would find a dolt trying to grab my hand on the street , followed by my wasteful efforts trying to make him understand some basic human etiquettes.

I am 20 now , 7 odd years passed by . Today I stumbled upon the horrendous case of Priyanka Reddy and realised it's the same crime just new faces , same candle marches just new people , same hollow words just new government ,same eve teasing just new places . One thing is new , my mind is screaming two questions now and they are :

1. WHY WOULD SOMEONE DO SUCH AN OBNOXIOUS THING?

2. WHEN WILL THIS SITUATION CHANGE?

Nikhil prajapati

I am Nikhil Prajapati from Faridabad haryana I am 18 years old I am student of 12 from commerce stream I started writing from October 2019, Writing is my hobby. Through the writting we can express our feelings andthis is my first book, I love Listening to music when i am happy or stressed.

Instagram ID: alfaaz_nikhil_k

कोख

जिस कोख से लिया है जन्म
उस कोख का मैं हमेशा कर्जदार रहूंगा
चाहे हो जाऊं मैं कितना भी अमीर
पर मैं यह कर्जन चुका सकूंगा
मां तूने मुझे दिखाई है यह दुनिया में हमेशा तेरा आभारी रहूंगा
जो मां तूमुझे छोड़कर गई तो मैं तेरे बिना कैसे रहूंगा
मुझे नहीं आती नींद इन मखमली गद्दो पे
आ जाती है नींद पड़ते ही मां की गोद में
मुझे नहीं चाहिए यह कोठी यह कार
बस मेरी मां का मुझ पर बरसता रहे प्यार
मां तू दुखी ना हो वरना मैं कमजोर पड़ जाऊंगा
हमेशा रह तू हंसती हुई फिर देख लियो मां तेरा आशीर्वाद ले आसमान भी छू जाऊंगा
बहुत आंसू दिए हैं इस मतलबी दुनिया ने मां अब तेरी आंखों में आंसू आने नहीं दूंगा
देखकर अपने बेटे की सफलता मां तू खुश हुई है अब तेरे चेहरे से खुशी जाने ना दूंगा
अब तेरे चेहरे से खुशी जाने ना दूंगा
जिस कोख से लिया है जन्म
उस कोख का मैं हमेशा कर्जदार रहूंगा
चाहे हो जाऊं मैं कितना भी अमीर
पर मैं यह कर्ज न चुका सकूंगा।

जिंदगी

यह जिंदगी पता नहीं कैसा खेल खेल रही है

एक परेशानी खत्म नहीं होती दूसरी लेकर आ रही है

मैं कोशिश करता हूं खुशियां ढूंढने की

यह जिंदगी मुझसे खुशियां छुपाए जा रही है

मैं जिंदगी के इस खेल से बोर हो गया हूं

दुख सहन करने के मामले में माहिर हो गया हूं

कोई तो लाकर दे दो मुझे कुछ खुशी

कैसी होती है खुशी में खुशी का चेहरा भूल गया हूं

मेरी जिंदगी में आता है हर कोई खुशी देने के बहाने से

देकर के वह मुझे दुख चला जाता है

अब कोई आएगा खुशी लेकर मैं उसे मना कर दूंगा आने से

मुझसे अब और कोई दुख नहीं सहा जाता है

कर लिए थे मैंने अपनी जिंदगी में पराए अपने और अपने कर लिए थे बेरी

कर लिया जो इतना बड़ा गुनाह इस गुनाह की सजा भी तो मिलनी थी मुझे जरूरी

क्यों करूं मैं अपनी जिंदगी से शिकायत यह तो अपना फर्ज निभा रही है

दे कर के मुझे दुख कौन अपना कौन पराया इसका एहसास करवा रही है

इस जिंदगी में कोई नहीं हो सकता पराया अपना जिंदगी मुझे यही बात समझा रही है

निखिल धन्यवाद करता है जिंदगी तेरा तेरे दिए हुए दुखों से से बात समझ आ गई सारी है।

अपने से ज्यादा प्यार करूंगा

आसमान से तारे तो तोड़ नहीं सकता

पर जितना हो सके तुझे खुश रखूंगा

ईतना प्यार कोई नहीं करता होगा

जितना प्यार जान मैं तुझे करूंगा

साथ छोड़कर मैं तेरा ना जाऊंगा

मरते दम तक मैं तुझे ही चाहूंगा

तू एक बार हां तो कर दे

तेरे लिए मैं दुनिया से लड़जाऊंगा

जो भी होंगे तेरे सपने अधूरे

उन सबको मैं पूरा करूंगा

निखिल की वजह से आए तेरी आंखों में आंसू

मैं कभी ऐसा कोई काम नहीं करूंगा

बस तू रहे हंसती मुस्कुराती हुई

उस खुदा से यही दुआ करूंगा

चाहे आइए तुझ पर कोई भी मुसीबत

तेरे आगे ढाल बनकर खड़ा रहूंगा

तेरे बदन से नहीं तेरी रूह से प्यार करूंगा

हीर रांझा की तरह अपनी मोहब्बत भी मशहूर करूंगा।

Pooja Negi

Pooja Negi loves to spill her emotions on pages. All she wants is to make her parents proud.

हवाएँ भी कुछ कहती हैं,

सुनना ज़रा कभी गौर से,

यूँही नहीं खुशबू फैलाते पुष्प,

मस्त पवन के जोर से,

तितलियों का शोर भी,

राग कोईन यागाता है,

यूँही नहीं, पंछियों का,

शोर गुनगुनाता है।

कवियित्री सच्ची

भारी शब्दों का मुझे ज्ञान नहीं,

सरल शब्दों से मेरा नाता है।

अपने जज्बातों को लिखकर, कह सकूँ,

मुझे बस,

वही शब्द समझ में आताहै।

कोई मेरी लेखनी को समझे नादानी, कोई समझे, अभी है बच्ची।

सचमें, इस बात का मुझे फर्क नहीं पड़ता,

मैं तो बस हूँ, एक कवि सच्ची।।

एक ऐसा मंजर

आज सुबह बंद आँखों से,

मैंने एक, ऐसा मंजर देखा,

हम खुद को खुद से मार रहे,

एक ऐसा खंजर देखा।

वीरानी सड़कें और वीराने घर बार थे,

सारी बिल्डिंग, सारी सुविधा,

सब खाली बेकार थे।

एक भी पंछी, एक भी प्राणी,

दूर दूर तक कुछ ना पास था,

एक भी पेड़ नहीं जमीं पर,

ये कैसा अद्भुत विकास था।

ज़रा सोचना तुम सब भी,

ये कैसी मोहमाया है?

अपनी ही प्रकृती को खत्मकर,

हमने खुद पर भारी संकट लाया है।

Pardeep Kumar Bogra

Pardeep Kumar Bogra, a software consultant and a spiritual seeker. Learning music these days, want to transform my life using this skill.

Instagram ID: PardeepBogra

(Life: Truth, Honesty, Love, Peace)

When we start living truthful & honest life, it is just a beginning. When we start thinking or talking about truthful and honest life, we are just exploring possibilities.

To be truthful, honest no one needs any guidance/guru. Once we become truthful, honest; everything looks so clear, we don't feel need for any guidance.

People who spread hate and violence, they also want/need love and peace to relax.

Stock of happiness is not limited; we don't need to give pain to others to be happy.

(Behavior and Character)

Expressing ourselves is good; sometimes keeping in mind/heart is good. What/how/when we express and keep in mind/heart, defines our character.

Exposing ourselves is more important than exposing others. Let others expose your mistakes, let others feel your goodness. We need to see do we really did those mistakes, do we really deserve praise! Why, When, How do we criticize/praise others defines our character!!!

Everyone expects results from others, how many of us do efforts for it. What others are doing, does not impact us; what are our own efforts, brings result for us.

What we see/understand outside depends on what we have inside..!!

#InnerWorld #wisdom #OuterWorld

(Me : Innerself, Introspection)

Over-confidence and underestimating ourselves; both are signs of moving in wrong direction. We should understand ourselves better to walk/move in right direction!

It is easy to speak truth about wrong/bad deeds of others, speaking truth about our own bad deeds and accepting mistakes by heart is real truthfulness.

If we follow good thoughts/leader(s) by heart, it impacts our soul for betterment; if we follow to show-off, it has adverse impact on our soul.

No one is watching me when I am doing wrong, if few are watching me they are also doing wrong, I have no fear. Our deeds has impact on state of our soul, it is inside our body.

If we stay strong during setbacks, it becomes milestone of our life! #setbacks #staystrong #milestone

Pragati Yadav

मेरा नाम प्रगति यादव है और मैं उत्तर प्रदेश के एटा जिले से हूँ मैं काफी सालों से लिखती आ रही हूँ लेकिन मेरी कविताएं पहली बार किसी किताब का हिस्सा बनी हैं। शुक्रिया।

Instagram ID: pragatipoetrys

The Silence of Ignited Souls

एक परिंदा टूट कर

सम्भलने लगा है

पंख पर मरहम लगा

उड़ने लगा है

अँधेरों से दूर

रोशनी में जा खडा़ है

एक परिंदा टूटकर

सम्भलने लगा है

अश्कों में डूबा

अब तैरने लगा है

दर्द गहरी चोटों का

भरने लगा है

बेअद बजुबां से

मुस्कुराने लगा है

बिखरकर फिर से

वजूद समेटने लगा है

एक परिंदा टूटकर

सम्भलने लगा है

बस इतनी रोशनी चाहिए

कि पाँव धर सकूँ

अपने लफ्जों को उतारकर

कुछ घाव भर सकूँ

बस इतनी रागिनी चाहिए

कि महसूस कर सकूँ

दुनिया के फसादों से

खुद को महफ़ूज़ रख सकूँ

बस इतनी चाँदनी चाहिए

कि चाँद निहार सकूँ

तन्हा सितारों को

खुद के नाम कर सकूँ

खुद को जान ले तू

ये मेरा ख्याल है

जिंदगी हँस पड़ेगी

वक्त की क्या मजाल है

जो बीत गया, जाने दो

किस्मत का क्यूँ मलाल है

खुद को जान ले तू

ये मेरा ख्याल है

बचा खुद को तू, यहाँ

हर कदम पर जाल है

डर है कि सहार का

तू खुद ही बेमिसाल है

जलने दे तू वो, जो

तेरे सीने में मशाल है

खुद को बस जान ले तू

ये मेरा ख्याल है

Promita Dey

I am Promita Dey, a simple girl who just trys to turn her emotions and feelings into words of lullaby and ink them on a piece of paper. I am student of University of Engineering and Management, Kolkata. Being a proud "Bengali", I certainly know how a piece of literature can bring a change in the world.

Instagram ID: _unspoken_girl

The Silence of Ignited Souls

I see them in awe; colourful uniforms,

Red and blue pencil pouches, many-hued crayons,

Tainted by cupidity, I pity for myself,

They play all around in their lavish bungalow,

And I sit there moping their floors.

I witness shelling every day and night,

They stop me on the way and say;

They target schools with heavy weaponary,

I feel shackled under my own home.

I want to read and learn, but to stay alive is what I yearn.

I wore a blue uniform and ran towards the classroom,

But it was empty as usual,

I kept dreaming the toffee jars, my favourite yellow cars,

And the time flew just like the vanishing morning dew,

I stare at the chair everyday; still noone turns up to make me read
and write.

I was the youngest in my house,

I used to run like my brothers; play and eat just like them,

But then every morning I remained at home cutting vegetables,

The Silence of Ignited Souls

And they jumped away with their bags to school,

Do you call it, "Gender disparity" or my father's will for my early marriage?

Being a son, I worked hand-in-hand with my father,

Somedays bearing cement sacks,

And somedays cleaning the gutter,

But every noon, I ran to school, just for the mid-day meals,

I wanted to learn, but it was outweighed always by the immediate need to earn.

You didn't win the game,

You didn't make the cut,

You didn't get the vote,

Your dreams went splat,

Oh! So they think you're a loser?

"You are a born-loser!",

They tell you are doomed to failure,

From the very start of life,

You tell them, it never mattered you win or lose,

The Silence of Ignited Souls

What mattered, is how you played the game!

We lose things all time,

We lose keys, money, socks,

We lose our loved one,

We suffer losses that bruises our ego,

Does losing make us losers?

Learning to live mean learning to lose,

That little loss will keep inspiring you,

To keep going, to keep trying,

To teach you to turn manure into fuel,

To dust yourself off and move again.

So, to the one who couldn't win the Oscar,

To the one who didn't win the election,

To the one who didn't fulfill his ambition at first try,

To the one who couldn't win the match,

You lost, but you aren't a loser!

Pratham Singla

A Driving Enthusiast, Introvert & Damaged But a Positive Person Who Is "Trying To Escape From Darkness" And Always Ready To Do And Explore Something New, Shopping Lover.I Write What My Heart Speak To Me And I Always Try To Give My Best In Every Opportunities I Get.

Instagram ID: soultalks.1131 & pratham_s283

The Silence of Ignited Souls

"Mai Mohobaat Nahi Badalta"

Maii Apni Mohobaat Badalta Nahi hun.,

Ek Jagah Sajda Karne Ke Baad Srr Jhukaata Vhii Hun,

Mujhe Nhi ShauQ Har Jagah Minnatein Karne Ka,

Mai Ek Daaman Jo Thaam Lun Phir Rehta Vhi hun..!!

"Vishwas Dilaane Waalon Par Vishwas Na Karo"

Vishwas Dilaane wale Hi Karte 'VishwasGhat',

Vishwas DilaaNe waalon Par Vishwas na kro,

Mohobaat Karne wale Hi Tode Mohobaat Ki Lakeer,

Inke Reet-e-Reewazo Par Tum Vishwas Na karo..,

Kab Kon Badal Jaye Apni Baaton Se Mukar Jaaye ..."Kiska Pta"?

Kab Kon Badal Jaye Apni Baaton Se Mukar Jaaye ..."Kiska Pta"?

The Silence of Ignited Souls

Tum 'Ro-Ro' Kar Kisi Ki Wajah Se Khud Ko Barbaad Na
Karo..!!

Kitnee Hi Zakhm De Le Tu Aee Mere Yaar.,

Chahat Kabhi Meri Kam Nahi Hogi.,

Chahunga Isi Kadar Tujhe Apni Aakhiri Saans Tak.,

Tujhse Juda Kabhi Ye Meri Rooh Nahi Hogi,

Talab Rahegi Har Dafa Terii,

Tere Sukoon Ko Ye Dil Tadpega..

Tu Mile Ya Na Mile Par..,

Mera Dil to Hmesha Sirf Tere Liye Hi Dhadkega.!!

Na Khud Ka Kuch Pata ..Na Saanson Ki Kuch Khabar Hai..,

Laakho Armaan Liye ..Soona Mera Ghar Hai.,

Ishq Beshumaar Or Wafa Gazab Ki Kee Hai Humne.,

Sb Kuch bhula baithaa hu..

Bs In Aankhon Mei Tumhare Laut Aane Ki Ummed Hai..!!

Dard Bharii Haii Zindagi ..Chaaro Taraf Gumo Ka Mela Hai,

Mt Ja Bande Is Mele Mei ..Sarphira Tu Akela Hai..,

Nikal Na Payega Phir Kabhii Is Mele Se Phaskr Khda Ho Jayega..,

Udja Bande Khule Aasmaan Mei ..Yahan Har jagah Maut Ka Ghera Hai..!!

Raja singh

Zindagi main logo ka parichay janna se acha hai ki unke swabhav janaa jaye kyuki waqt ke sath logo ka parichay badal jata hai par unka swabhav zindagi bhar nahi badalta.

Instagram ID: rajabhaiya3847

ज़िन्दगी एक शब्द भी है और एक एहसास भी है और एक खुशी भी है और एक दुख भी है और त्याग भी है और उपहार भी है।

ज़िन्दगी को हम तीन नजरियों से देख सकते है, जब एक शिशु इस दुनिया में जन्म लेता है पर उसके जन्म से नौ महीने पूर्व जन्म लेती है एक मां। और उस मां के द्वारा जो त्याग किए जाते है वो कुछ इस प्रकार है-

सुंदरता :- एक कन्या के लिए सुंदरता उसका सबसे विशेष गुण होती है और चाहे वे आंतरिक सुंदरता हो या बाहरी सुंदरता। किन्तु एक मां का उत्तरदायित्व निभाने के लिए वो इन सभी प्रकार की सामग्रियों का त्याग कर देती है जिससे उसके नवजात शिशु को किसी प्रकार की हानि ना पहुंच सके। और एक मा अपने शिशु के लिए, अपने गहने, लिपस्टिक, काजल, क्रीम, पाउडर आदि चीजों का त्याग कर देती है क्योंकि एक मां अपने बच्चो को कभी कोई भी परेशानी में नहीं देख सकती। और अगर कोई परेशानी उसके बच्चे पर आती भी है तो वे उस परेशानी को अपने ऊपर ले जाती है और अपने बच्चे को उस परेशानी का एहसास तक नहीं होने देती क्युकी एक मां तो मां ही होती है।

त्याग :- एक मां अपने बच्चे की पसंद के लिए और उसके मानव रूपी शरीर के साथ, विकास की और अपने कदम बढ़ाते हुए चलती जाती है। और उन लोगो का अपनी ज़िन्दगी में त्याग करती चली जाती है जो उसके बच्चे को पसंद नहीं करते है। और वो अपने शिशु को लड़खड़ाते हुए और उसके नन्हे मुनने कदमों के साथ हमेशा उसको गिरने से बचाती है क्युकी वो जानती है चोट तो उसके शिशु को आएगी पर फिर दर्द उस मां को होगा। और दुनिया कि हर एक मां महान है क्युकी वो अपने बच्चे पर आने वाली हर परेशानी को अपने ऊपर ले जाती है और उस शिशु को परेशानी का एहसास तक नहीं होने देती। क्युकी मां तो मां ही होती है।

द्वितीयचरण

जब शिशु बोलने चलने और विचारो को समझना शुरू करता है और इस दुनिया में और दूसरे बच्चो और लोगो के साथ रहकर अपना विकास करने योग्य हो रहा

होता है तो इस वक़्त, उस मा को सबसे ज्यादा चिंता सताती है पर उसको इस बात की चिंता भी अधिक सताती है कि कहीं वो बच्चा किसी गलत संगत में ना पड़ जाए या उसकी मां के लिए उसका प्यार कम ना हो जाए क्युकी अब वो हर वक़्त अपनी मां के साथ नहीं होगा और उसको हर रोज उसकी ज़िन्दगी में नए लोग मिलेंगे पर उसको इस बात से सबसे अधिक भय लगता है कि कहीं कोई उसके बच्चे को हट ना कर दे । और उसको रुला ना दे । और क्युकी अब वो हर वक़्त उसके साथ उसके आशु रोकने के लिए नहीं होगी। और उसको इस बात का एहसास भी होता है कि अब उसके और उसके बच्चे के बीच के रिश्ते में बहुत सारे लोग आने वाले है क्युकी जो छोटी छोटी बातें वो अपनी मां को बताया करता था वो अब उसके नए दोस्तों को बताई जाएगी। और जब वो बच्चे और मां एक दूसरे के साथ खाना खाया करते थे अब पता नहीं कितने दिनों में यह पल उस मां की ज़िन्दगी में आया करेगा। पर वो मां यह एहसास किसी को नहीं बताती। क्युकी उस मां को सिर्फ अपने बच्चे की खुशी ही प्यारी लगती है, क्युकी मां तो मां होती है।

तृतीयचरण

जब उस बच्चे की ज़िन्दगी में एक मा की अहमियत सिर्फ एक ख्याल रखने वाले इंसान की हो जाती है, जिस समय उस बच्चे को, ना तो उसे अपनी मा के साथ खाना खाना जरूरी लगता है और ना अपनी मां के साथ अपनी ज़िन्दगी की बातों को बताना। जब उस बच्चे की ज़िन्दगी में वो लोग जरूरी हो जाते है जिनके लिए ना तो वो जरूरी होता है और ना ही कभी होगा, पर फिर भी वो बच्चा उस मायावी दुनिया के लोगों के पीछे भागता है जो अपने को अपनों से दूर करना और ज़रूरत के वक़्त लोगो का साथ छोड़ना और बुरे वक़्त में लोगो का मज़ाक उड़ाना जानते है पर जब तक उस बच्चे को इस बात का एहसास होता है कि वो मां होती थी। जो रातो को ठंड में जागकर उसको कम्बल उड़ाया करती थी और उसके बच्चे की तबयत खराब होने पर पूरी रात सोती नहीं थी और उस बच्चे के बिना कुछ कहे उसके चेहरे को दुख से सुख में परिवर्तित कर देती थीं क्युकी मां तो मां ही होती है।

नोट:- जो भी इस मैसेज को पढ़ चुके है उनसे हाथ जोड़कर एक विनती है ज़िन्दगी में अपने पीछे भीड़ लेकर चलने से अच्छा है अपनी मां के साथ चलिए, जिसने कभी आपको गिरने नहीं दिया और अगर गिर भी गए तो आपको कभी दर्द का एहसास तक नहीं होने दिया।

द मदर इज गॉडगिफ्टेड

Saba Parvez

A fervent writer who knows how to pen down her sentiments on those deadpan sheets!

Instagram ID: deperilme

To what extent is it appropriate to unravel your universe in black and white when there is so much more beneath the greys!!

#Darkness!!

The one of our nethermost oblique,

The one in which those gleaming stars shimmer,

The one holding our lurid secrets,

The one which brace reticence even in growling bearings,

The one who avail those feral wolves to adore that moon's sight,

The one which grant those fireflies to blaze and rejoice honest affection,

The one which always endorse us to deem our retentive times,

The one which reprieve even when we splinter ourselves to survive,

The one which smuggle solely in clement daytime,

The one which doesn't inflict yet some are afraid,

Yeah, 'darkness' one which evils out the dark!!

घाट किनारे बैठे आज ज़रा हताश नज़र आते हो,

आँखों में यूँ अशक भरे किस्से किसके लहरों से खुस-फुसाते हो।

ये किसके टूटे बिखरे ख्वाब बार बार पिरोये जाते हो,

आखिर है कौन वो,

जिसकी यादो में डूबे बे-लौस से मालूम पाते हो।।

Dear World,

I'm no more a Cinderella. Coz I don't have to wait for my Prince Charming to come over and make my dreams come true. I'm worth conquering them myself. And the countdown to my success starts now!!

Yours Lovingly!

A dark unlit sky,

Setting snuggly under the night,

Glimmer of stars above,

With our cokes resting on our sides,

An ideal date of mine,

Those sharing memories,

While forging one with you,

The Silence of Ignited Souls

Our favourite song reaching to our ears,

From the car's radio,

Pouring in the background,

Merging with serenity gently,

An ideal date of mine,

A sudden gust of wind,

In that gratifying ambiance,

Then the way you dragged me closer,

To that amorous dance,

Me sinking in your mild blue eyes,

Embraced in your arms,

The darkness vanishing in the dawn,

An ideal date of mine!!

Shivani Tripathi

My name is Shivani Tripathi. I'm from Prayagraj. My father Mr. Anil Kumar Tripathi is an accountant and mother Mrs. Kamlesh Kumari is a skilled housewife. Currently pursuing Bachelor of Education from Allahabad University. I have been very close to nature since childhood and from there I got inspiration to write. I love writing poems and writing articles.. I thank to my Friend's Teacher's Parent's & lord Krishna for everything. I'm a creative person who loves adventure.

उसने कहा था मुझे . . . . .

उसने कहा था मुझे . .

आंखों मैं काजल लगाया करो

अपनी जुल्फों को संवारा करो

काली छोटी सी बिंदी सजाया करो

होठों की लाली न हटाया करो

पलकों को झुकाकर शर्माया करो

अपनी हंसी की खिलखिलाहट बिखराया करो

अच्छी लगती हो ! ! !

तुम्हारे आंखों की प्यारी सी चमक

गुलाबी गालों पर काले तिल ,

सुर्ख होठों पर प्यारी सी मुस्कान

हाथों की खनकती चूड़ी और माथे की बिंदियां

कमी है तो एक चुटकी सिंदूर की

वरना बिखरे बालों के बीच तुम

बेहद अच्छी लगती हो ! ! !

पूर्ण विराम . . . . . .

कभी आ कर मिलो मुझसे इस कदर

मेरी रूह तक महका जाओ।

ना बिछड़ने का डर हो थोड़ा

ऐसे गले से लगा जाओ।

क्यों तड़पाते हो आकर बार - बार

खुद को मुझमें मिला जाओ।

मैं जो हूं रहूं ने मिलकर वह

तुम जादू कोई चला जाओ।

आंखें बरस रही है झर - झर

थोड़ा तो सुकून दिल आ जाओ।

ना हो इश्क अगर तुम्हें मुझसे

झूठा ही प्यार जता जाओ।।

मेरी आखिरी ख्वाहिश समझ कर ही

नजरें नजरों से मिला जाओ।

मैं नहीं किसी की हूं कान्हा

तुम तो आक रअपना जाओ।

तरसी हूं हर पल दर्शन को

आंखों की प्यास बुझा जाओ।

मिल जाओ मुझे हे मुरलीधर !

या मझधार से पार लगा जाओ।

तुम भी सुनोगे जो दिल की मेरे

मेरी सांसो को उजड़ा जाओ।

बहुत हुआ घुट – घुट कर जीना

जीवन पर पूर्ण विराम लगा जाओ।

बेवजह जुड़ गई हूं तुझसे इतना कि

सांसे छूटे तो छोटे तू साथ हर पल रहे . .

में रहूं चाहे जिस शहर जिस गली

तेरे नाम की हवा मुझे छूकर गुजरे।

घिर जाएं घटाएं सावन की

रिमझिम – रिमझिम बरसात गिरे . .

मैं भीगूं तेरे आगोश में आकर

तन मन हर्षित होकर खिले।

तेरे नाम से धड़कनों का बढ़ जाना

तेरा मुझसे ही लिपटना मुस्काना . . .

तेरी बातों की खनक जादू वो नशा

तेरी रूह से रूह का मिल जाना।

नामें रिश्तो में बंधी कोई नाम लिए

न मोहताज हूं किसी के फरमान की

मैं स्वतंत्र हूं प्रेयसी , प्रेमिका तेरी

ईश्वर पर कर विश्वास लिए अरमान थी |

मुझे क्या पता था बिखर जाऊंगी

सोचा था कि प्यार पाकर निखर जाऊंगी

अरमान भी टूटा विश्वास भी टूटा ,

जिसे पूरी जिंदगी चाहा उसे उसी का साथ भी छूटा . . जाते – जाते वह ऐसे कदमों में बांध गया

सपनों को तोड़ा , हृदय को निचोड़ा . .

आंखों के आंसुओ को भी वो

बेदर्दी से सुखा गया।

Shivi saxena

Mr. Vinod saxena and Mrs. Ranjana saxena

Shivi is a 17 year old girl who is passionate about reading books. She loves to write short quotes and poems. She believes in being kind and radiate positivity, from her perspective life should be meaningful even if it's short.

"I dedicate my write-ups to my parents, showing my gratitude towards my beloved ones. This was my surprise for you. I love you a lots mumma papa"

All I have

I have my dad who stands by my side supporting me through my rough time, helping me stand on my feet, telling me it will be okay, just don't cry.

I have my mom who appreciates all my little efforts , taking care of me as I'm a little child., scolding me just to make me smile.

I can never have the correct words to tell my feelings to my lifelines. Even if I try , a million 'I love you' won't be ever enough to show the love that I have stored for them in the deep center of my heart. Even a small hug from them makes me cry.

You both are all I have. That's all I have.

She's a happy girl. With a heart like black hole, taking her soul with every disappointment and heartbreak.

I want a love that will last lifelong,

A love to cherish, smile, to fight for.

A love that will heal my soul, stay by my side even if all odds went horribly wrong.

I hope to have a love like this, by my side, when I'm about to close my eyes.

A love like this is worth waiting for, even if it exists, just in my thoughts.

Sneha Mishra

Sneha Mishra. Student of class 10th. I pen down my imagination.

THE CAGED GIRL.

It has been years now

Since the girl is caged

In her own house

By her own people

She can see the beauty

She can see the sky

But can't fly high

She looks the world

Dreaming to be a part

But can't for her dreams

They are teared apart

She is smiling to

Hide her tears

She is laughing to

Hide her pain

But reality is

Sucking her vein.

She seems to be alive but

She is dead with

Her breaths in her hand!!

गलत आदमी ही नहीं

उसका समय भी होता है।

बुरा आदमी ही नहीं,

उसके हालात भी होते है।

मतलबी आदमी ही नहीं,

उसकी तकदीर भी होती है।

और कमजोर आदमी ही नहीं,

उसके हौसले भी होते है।

Doesn't matter how small your dreams are,

You should always plan big to achieve them...